Monet's Cat

By **Lily Murray**

Illustrated by **Becky Cameron**

RANDOM HOUSE STUDIO ■ NEW YORK

Monet was a famous painter with
a magic cat. Her name was Chika.

She was made of delicate pottery,
and lay on a cushion, cool and still, until . . .

. . . Monet tapped her three times with his paintbrush.
Then Chika came alive!

She yawned and st r e t c h e d...

...and opened her eyes.

Time for an adventure!

But it was too wet to go outside.

So she set off down the corridor.

"Chika?" called Monet.
"Where are you off to?"

"Are you getting up
to mischief again?"

But Chika wasn't under the table.

Or on the chair.

"Where could she be?"
Then Monet spotted her...

...inside his painting.

"Chika!" said Monet. "Come out of there."
But Chika wasn't listening.
"Oh dear." Monet sighed. "Here we go."

Monet stood in the sunshine, breathing
in the rich scent of summer flowers.

"I remember painting this," he said.
"We'd all had a delicious lunch. And there's Jean,
my son, playing with his blocks of wood.
But where is Chika?"

Chika crept out from under the
tablecloth and leapt onto the table.

She lapped milk
from a teacup.

She nibbled on a
piece of crusty bread.

"Hey!" yelled Jean. "A naughty cat is eating our lunch. Don't worry—I'll catch her."

But Chika was too fast for him.

"Wait, Chika!"
said Monet. But Chika was already leaping out of the picture . . .

. . . and Monet came t u m b l i n g after.

"Oh no! Not again." Monet sighed.
He was too late. Chika was on to the next painting.

Monet jumped in after her and landed with a bump.
Around him, people ran this way and that.

"Where am I?" Monet wondered for a moment.
Then, hearing a deafening Choooo! Chooooo! he knew...
"The station at Saint-Lazare. The thrill of the engines.
The clanking metal. The rushing feet."

He was surrounded by steam and smoke,
billowing up toward the great arched roof.

"But where is Chika?"

She was dancing between
clouds of steam.

Monet raced after her, puffing
and panting, weaving in and
out of busy crowds.

"Stop that cat!"
called the stationmaster,
blowing his whistle.

Then Monet saw her—on a train.

"Get down, Chika! You don't even have a ticket."

"Where will she go next . . . ?"

"The seaside!" said Monet, sitting
for a moment to catch his breath.

Flags fluttered, parasols twirled, and clouds raced
across the sky . . . and Monet began to smile.
There was something about the seaside
that always made him feel holiday-ish.

Chika's tail twitched with excitement.

She prowled.

She pounced.

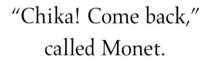 "Chika! Come back,"
called Monet.

  "Got you."

They shared an ice cream on the sand.
"I don't want our adventure to end quite yet,"
said Monet. "Let's visit one more painting."

"This," said Monet, "is one of my favorite places in the world. I could paint the lily pond forever—the water, the flowers, the green-blue leaves. It's so peaceful."

But Chika had spotted something . . .

Monet looked down just as she landed
with a tremendous SPLASH

right in the middle of the lily pond.

"Yowl!" cried Chika.

"Oh, Chika." Monet chuckled, scooping her up. "Let's go home."

Monet looked back at his paintings.
They were in a terrible mess.

As for Chika, she put her tail in the air
and padded back to her favorite spot.

Monet found her curled up in a sunbeam, her eyes closed.

"I think you've made enough mischief for one day," said Monet, and he tapped her three times with his paintbrush.

At once, Chika became very cool and still.

Outside, the sun was beginning to set across the sky.
"What beautiful light." Monet picked up his paints.
"Sweet dreams, Chika," he whispered. "Until next time . . ."

The Luncheon, 1874

The Boardwalk on the Beach at Trouville, 1870

Bridge over a Pond of Water Lilies, 1899

The Gare St.-Lazare, 1877

The True Story of Monet's Cat

Chika, the magic cat, is based on a real pottery cat that was
given to Monet as a present. The pottery cat spent many years
in Monet's house in Giverny, France, curled up on a cushion.

The cat was later spotted in the home of Michel, Monet's second son.
But after his death, it seemed to vanish. In fact, Michel had given the cat to
his daughter, Rolande Verneiges, along with many of Monet's paintings.

The cat wasn't seen again for many years, and people thought it had been lost forever.
Then, in 2018, an art expert from Christie's, a British auction house, visited Rolande's
daughter in her apartment. There, he spotted the white pottery cat sitting on a piano.

A Japanese art collector bought the ornament and kindly donated it to the
Claude Monet Foundation, which keeps Monet's house in Giverny open to visitors.

Today, Monet's cat is back at Giverny, peacefully sleeping on a cushion
in the dining room. Perhaps she is dreaming of her next adventure…

For Freya —L.M.
For Andrew —B.C.

Text copyright © 2020 by Michael O'Mara Books Limited
Jacket art and interior illustrations copyright © 2020 by Becky Cameron
All rights reserved. Published in the United States by Random House Studio, an imprint of Random House Children's Books,
a division of Penguin Random House LLC, New York.
Originally published in paperback by Michael O'Mara Books Limited, London, in 2020.
Random House Studio and the colophon are registered trademarks of Penguin Random House LLC.
Page 30: *The Luncheon,* 1874 (Gianni Dagli Orti/Shutterstock) Page 31 (l–r): *The Gare St.-Lazare,* 1877 (Granger/Shutterstock); *Bridge over a Pond of Water Lilies,* 1899
(Gianni Dagli Orti/Shutterstock); *The Boardwalk on the Beach at Trouville,* 1870 (Universal History Archive/UIG/Shutterstock) Page 32: Photograph © Martin Bailey
Visit us on the Web! rhcbooks.com Educators and librarians, for a variety of teaching tools, visit us at RHTeachersLibrarians.com
Library of Congress Cataloging-in-Publication Data is available upon request.
ISBN 978-0-593-30613-0 (trade) — ISBN 978-0-593-30614-7 (lib. bdg.) — ISBN 978-0-593-30615-4 (ebook)

MANUFACTURED IN CHINA 10 9 8 7 6 5 4 3 2 1 First Edition
Random House Children's Books supports the First Amendment and celebrates the right to read.